THIS BOOK
BELONGS TO:

_____

_____

_____

For Anna
M.W.

For Sebastian,
David & Candlewick
H.O.

Published by arrangement with Walker Books Ltd, London SE11 5HJ

Dual language edition first published 2006 by Mantra Lingua
Dual language TalkingPEN edition first published 2010 by Mantra Lingua
Global House, 303 Ballards Lane, London N12 8NP, UK
http://www.mantralingua.com

Text copyright © 1991 Martin Waddell
Illustrations copyright © 1991 Helen Oxenbury
Dual language text and audio copyright © 2006 Mantra Lingua
This edition 2018

A CIP record of this book is available from the British Library

Printed in Paola, Malta MP190718PB08180382

鸭子农夫

FARMER DUCK

written by
MARTIN WADDELL

illustrated by
HELEN OXENBURY

Mantra Lingua

从前有一只鸭子，它很不幸地与一个懒惰的老农夫一起住。
鸭子要做所有的工作，而农夫则整天懒卧在床上。

There once was a duck who had the bad luck
to live with a lazy old farmer.
The duck did the work.
The farmer stayed
all day in bed.

鸭子从耕地把牛拉回。
「工作做得怎样？」农夫叫道，
鸭子回答说：
「嘎！」

The duck fetched the cow from the field.
"How goes the work?"
called the farmer.
The duck answered,
"Quack!"

鸭子从山丘上把羊群带领回来。
「工作做得怎样？」农夫叫道，
鸭子回答说：
「嘎！」

The duck brought the sheep from the hill.
"How goes the work?" called the farmer.
The duck answered,
"Quack!"

鸭子把鸡只们赶回它们的鸡屋。
「工作做得怎样？」农夫叫道，
鸭子回答说：
「嘎！」

The duck put the hens in their house.
"How goes the work?"
called the farmer.
The duck answered,
"Quack!"

农夫由于整天睡觉而变得肥胖，
可怜的鸭子则因为整天工作而逐渐感到厌烦。

The farmer got fat through staying in bed
and the poor duck got fed up
with working all day.

「工作做得怎样？」
「嘎！」

"How goes the work?"
"QUACK!"

「工作做得怎样？」
「嘎！」

"How goes the work?"
"QUACK!"

「工作做得怎样？」
「嘎！」

"How goes the work?"
"QUACK!"

「工作做得怎样？」
「嘎！」

"How goes the work?"
"QUACK!"

「工作做得怎样？」
「嘎！」

"How goes the work?"
"QUACK!"

「工作做得怎样？」
「嘎！」

"How goes the work?"
"QUACK!"

可怜的鸭子泪汪汪的，
又疲乏，又想睡。

The poor duck was sleepy
and weepy
and tired.

鸡只们、羊群和牛都感到很不安，
它们都喜爱鸭子，
于是它们便在月亮下开了一个会，
为第二天的早晨作好计划。

「哞！」牛说，
「咩！」羊群说，
「咯！」鸡只们说。
那便是它们的计划了。

The hens and the cow
and the sheep got very
upset.
They loved the duck.
So they held a meeting
under the moon and
they made a plan
for the morning.

"MOO!" said the cow.
"BAA!" said the sheep.
"CLUCK!" said the hens.
And THAT was the plan!

就在清晨之前，农场还很静寂，
牛、羊群、以及鸡只们悄悄地从后门走进屋子。

It was just before dawn and the farmyard was still.
Through the back door and into the house
crept the cow and the sheep and the hens.

它们偷偷地走过门堂，
吱吱嘎嘎地爬上楼梯。

They stole down the hall.
They creaked
up the stairs.

它们挤到农夫的床底下扭动，
那张床开始摇摆，农夫醒过来叫道：
「工作做得怎样？」
跟着…

They squeezed under the bed of
the farmer and wriggled about.
The bed started to rock and the
farmer woke up, and he called,
"How goes the work?"
and...

「哞！」
「咩！」
「咯！」

"MOO!"
"BAA!"
"CLUCK!"

它们将床抬起，农夫开始大声地叫喊，
它们敲撞著，把农夫抛来抛去，
将他从床上抛弹下来⋯

They lifted his bed and he started to shout, and they banged
and they bounced the old farmer about and about and about,
right out of the bed...

农夫逃跑去了，牛、羊群、以及鸡只们跟着他，
围着他哞呀、咩呀、咯呀地叫。

and he fled with the cow and the sheep and the hens mooing and baaing and clucking around him.

沿着小路⋯
「哞！」

Down the lane...
"Moo!"

穿过田间⋯
「咩！」

through the fields...
"Baa!"

越过山丘…
「咯！」

over the hill...
"Cluck!"

他再也不回来了。

and he never came back.

鸭子醒来后，蹒跚地走进农场，
以为会听到「工作做得怎样？」
但没有人说一句话！

The duck awoke and waddled wearily into the yard expecting
to hear, "How goes the work?"
But nobody spoke!

跟着牛、羊群、以及鸡只们都回来了。
「嘎？」鸭子问道，
「哞！」牛说，
「咩！」羊群说，
「咯！」鸡只们说。
它们将整件事告诉鸭子。

Then the cow and the sheep and the hens came back.
"Quack?" asked the duck.
"Moo!" said the cow.
"Baa!" said the sheep.
"Cluck!" said the hens.
Which told the duck
the whole story.

它们跟着便哞呀、咩呀、
咯呀和嘎呀地到农场工作去。

Then mooing and baaing
and clucking and quacking
they all set to work
on their farm.

Here are some other bestselling

dual language books from Mantra

Lingua for you to enjoy.